37780

THE WARLOCK
OF WESTFALL

THE

WARLOCK

OF

WESTFALL

Written and Illustrated by

Leonard Everett Fisher

Doubleday & Company, Inc.
Garden City, New York

ISBN: 0-385-07125-6
0-385-04476 Prebound
Library of Congress Catalog Card Number 73–82625

CONTENTS

PART ONE

THE ARREST

I

SAMUEL SWIFT sat on the edge of his rumpled bed listening to the last nervous sounds of the damp night disappear into the wilderness. The hot July sun still lay hidden over the eastern hills. Soon, it would rise and roast the sloping meadow nearby. Only Swift Pond, a large tree-shaded watery hole at the meadow's forested end, would remain cool, inviting.

The old man sat and half listened to the rasping voices of a million katydids, once so certain, so persistent, grow faint and vague. It was as if on command they had turned around and marched off in orderly platoons to disturb some other night in some other place; a vast crawling, crunching army, their whirring protest needed elsewhere. Here and there the resonant croak of a fat frog—or was it three or four?—interrupted the cadence of the marching katydids. A final hoot from an owl perched high in a leafy oak and it was all over. The night was done. It had gone away. Nothing was left. No moving shadow. No sound. Nothing. There was only the soft breathing of Samuel Swift in that dark void hovering between the going of night and the coming of day. In Samuel Swift's dazed consciousness, the room, at that moment, had no walls. It seemed to drop off into nowhere. And had Samuel Swift reached out in his dreamy imagination, he would have touched the end of the endless universe.

Old and sleepless Samuel Swift was motionless, waiting—waiting for the cock to crow, to shatter the peace, to wake up the new morning.

It did.

Now he stirred, creaked and slowly rose to add another day to his long, lonely life in the village of Westfall, Massachusetts, in the year of Our Lord, 1692.

Samuel shuffled to the door, lifted the iron latch and stepped outside. He chased a few chickens scratching in his carefully tended forget-me-nots and then peered intently toward the pond and woods. All he could see in the rising light were silhouetted treetops; while the morning mist floated low over the meadow and clung to the ground like a ghostly veil, hiding much of the landscape. In another hour or two, the warm sun would begin to melt the mist and reveal the quiet countryside. By noon, the clear fresh morning scene would waver and melt in a haze of summer heat. The still air would press the land and drive every living thing into cooler corners. This is the way it was yesterday and the day before and the week before that. And this is the way it would be tomorrow and the day after and the week ahead.

In such searing, windless summer calm, the Westfall villagers were becoming bored and restless. Their feverish minds smoldered and then burned with visions of the devil himself stoking the unrelenting fire around them.

"And why us, Dear Lord?" they asked.

And why not? Had not the devil together with his demons, witches and warlocks been overwhelming the rest of Massachusetts? Was not witchery in possession of nearby Salem? Had not numerous old hags already been brought to trial, condemned there and occasionally hanged by the neck for their sorcery? Why not Westfall?

"Where have we sinned, Dear Lord," the villagers cried out in despair. "Save us, Dear Lord," they pleaded in their meetinghouse. And then they all slumped forward on their long benches, too exhausted to resist; cooked in the sweltering heat of the meetinghouse; convinced that strong prayers alone could not keep them from the hellish broiling that soon would be theirs.

Samuel took another step, looked around and chased the chickens once more. A moment later he shuffled back inside the house to meet the scorching day and some of the village boys who would surely come to splash in the cool pond.

UNTIL a month ago, Samuel did not mind when the village boys—John Hayward, Richard Spencer, William Hampshire and a half dozen or so more—appeared in the pond. Village boys had been coming to the pond for years, especially when a summer day became a blazing caldron and there was little else to do. Samuel never kept them off the property—his property—given to him by the good people of Westfall for military services rendered fifty years before. The pond belonged to the spirited Westfall boys whenever they wanted it.

If Samuel happened to be in the pond when the boys arrived, he would float a safe distance away from all the splashing and quietly watch the fun. The boys paid little attention to him.

No, Samuel did not mind. He liked having all that youthful excitement around him. Usually, the young swimmers made such a racket that every woodland songbird would become silent with the wonder of it all. Having the boys there made Samuel feel young again—almost.

Once, Samuel felt younger than he should have. He had been watching the boys take turns jumping into the water feet first from a high overhanging tree limb. Before anybody had realized it, the skinny old man had climbed up the tree and crawled out to the end of the limb. There he slipped and lost his hold on the limb before he was ready to jump. Instead of breaking the water with his feet, he flattened it with his stomach and sank to the bottom half conscious. The boys pulled him out before he could drown and watched the gasping, wheezing Samuel stumble back up the meadow to the safety of the house. After that harrowing escapade, Samuel never again swam in the pond. It was then that the gloom of his unsteady old age—his once proud but lost vigor—settled over him and deepened with every passing day. Soon, his occasional hikes into the village along the straight half-mile trail became less frequent until they stopped altogether.

Finally, Samuel Swift's world became listless and hollow. His long interest in the unspoiled land and wildlife around him was not even a memory. He quit hunting, fishing and challenging the wilderness—the only things that fired his spirit and gave meaning to his life. It was as if the very soul of Samuel Swift had fled his body before its appointed hour. He ate sparingly, slept little, chopped some wood and gathered kindling for his fire, cleaned his ancient wheel lock musket over and over again and puttered with a few flowers. Except for sitting and staring, that was all he did.

He no longer had any real friends among the villagers. Those that he knew and counted on had long since passed on. One family had returned to England, beaten by the wilderness. Several families that were kind to him left Westfall long ago to begin again elsewhere down the New England coast. The rest simply did not live as long as he did. No new settlers had come to Westfall to replace those who had left or died. What remained in Westfall's small but swelling population were the children, grandchildren and great-grandchildren of those who broke away from Boston so many years before to stay and found their own religious community—their own style of Puritanism.

Samuel, never having married, unhappily felt no particular ties to the more recent generations of Westfallians. And for their part, the new generations regarded the aging hermit who lived at the far end of town as a crazy old fool who would have been much better off had he raised a family and become part of the day-to-day life of the village. At the very least, he probably might have attended religious services regularly. As it was, no one could remember ever seeing Samuel Swift inside the Westfall meetinghouse.

There was a time when some of the villagers actually prayed for Samuel's salvation. But that, too, was long ago. They finally gave up, declaring, "Samuel Swift has been stricken from the Lord's list. Samuel Swift will boil in hell!"

Samuel had become a stranger in their midst. Only the boys swimming in his pond gave the old man what meager companionship he craved—however distant. And now he no longer wanted them about.

In his constant solitude and growing loneliness, made more overwhelming when measured against the vastness of the uncivilized continent that enveloped him, Samuel began to despair for a family he never had and could no longer have. He filled his dreams with a wife that might have been; with children and grandchildren that should have been. Slowly, his wandering, desperate old mind conjured up visions of a Swift family that became a vivid reality. More and more, he was unable to separate the sharp picture of his dreams from the actual circumstance of his true situation. Real life became an illusion. And illusion—the dream of a family—however fanciful, became a stark reality. Old Samuel Swift had succeeded in making himself believe that he was, indeed, a family man.

Perhaps more startling was the fact that not only did Samuel Swift invent a family for himself, but in his dreamy, simple logic, he accounted for them by having them all dead and buried in the woods near his pond.

Actually, there were no real graves. Samuel

did not dig holes in the ground. He did nothing more during the past month than to crudely whittle the bare facts, as he had imagined them to be, on slabs of black walnut bark and set them into the damp earth:

ANNE SWIFT
WIFE
B. 1619—D. 1661
RIP

There were similar markers for David Swift, a son; Elizabeth Swift Newton, a daughter; her husband, John Newton; and two grandchildren, Baby Mary and Peter. Since according to the dates of their births and deaths, these supposed grandchildren never survived childhood—a common occurrence in early New England—and thus could hardly have married and produced children of their own, Samuel deprived himself of the distinction of having been a great-grandfather. Surely, he was old enough to have reached that advanced station. The thought simply never crossed his mind.

One final wood grave marker was added by the old man sometime during the previous restless night:

NATHAN SWIFT
BROTHER
B. 1607—D. 1692
RIP

Samuel seemed to have the presence of mind to do his "family" work at night rather than in

broad daylight to prevent discovery. In what must
have been a rare moment of clear thinking, he
had decided that these special activities should
be his secret. After all, family matters were pri-
vate and not subject to village gossip—especially
now that everyone in Massachusetts was looking
for the devil and his collaborators under every
blade of grass. The truth of the matter was that
Samuel had become aware of the possibility that
his Westfallian neighbors, already alarmed over
the appearance of witches in Salem, would come
to believe that he, Samuel Swift, a crazy old fool
to begin with, was possessed by demons and would
have to be dealt with accordingly. The prospect
was not pleasant. He could be arrested, tortured,
tried and convicted of sorcery. He might even
be put to death. Yet, he persisted in creating his
family—albeit, in the gloom of night. And now
that he had, he was just as stubbornly moved to
protect their final "resting place" from prying eyes
—especially the eyes of Westfall boys frolicking in
his pond not one hundred feet from the clearing
in the woods where the markers stood.

"Show me the demons," he would mutter over
and over again, "and I'll show you the freemen
of Westfall. Bah! To hell with them! May the
devil himself be on his guard when they arrive
in his palace below!"

In any event, the addition of Nathan Swift's
name to the list was a curious thing for a man
who chose not to recognize the difference between

who was real and who was not with regard to the emptiness of his personal life. The fact was that while his "deceased" wife, daughter, son, son-in-law and grandchildren were pure invention, giving Samuel a sense of belonging to someone, Nathan Swift was not wholly imaginary. Samuel did have a brother, Nathan, three years older than himself.

The last time these two had seen each other was on a Thames River dock in England sixty-two years back. However, in that long span of time, and considering the old man's craving and mental wanderings, it was difficult for him to remember Nathan as a real blood relation or, for that matter, whether there was any brother at all. If he did recognize Nathan's true existence, he could have assumed that he was dead, for in all those sixty-two years there was no communication whatever between them. Actually, Samuel had no clear idea about brother Nathan, real or not, one way or the other. Nathan just emerged somehow from deep within the mysterious workings and confusion of Samuel's tired brain. And since he did, Samuel simply committed him, like the others, to an eternity in the woods by placing a marker in the clearing which had become the "Swift burial ground."

All that Samuel had left to do was to transplant the forget-me-nots, growing near his house, to the foot of each of the six pieces of bark that marked the "graves" of his family. And this, too, would have to be done at night.

At the moment, Samuel's chief concern was the group of Westfall boys who would soon tramp past his house, race down the sloping meadow, tear off their clothes and jump into the cool pond. And now he was determined to keep them and anyone else away from the pond, away from the woods, away from his secret. Samuel took his gleaming old musket down from the fireplace wall. He leaned it carefully behind the open door of his house.

III

THE BLISTERING July sun had now risen higher in the cloudless sky. Once more Samuel came out of the house as the distant sounds of approaching boys drifted toward him.

"They're coming again. Damned nuisance they are, one and all. They'll not have my pond today or any day. Damned nuisance."

The sounds came closer. The old man now could distinguish the shouting, laughing and unmistakable authority of Johnnie Hayward who was leading the pack of sweaty youths to the pond.

"Say, there's old Swift."

"What's he waving for?"

"You don't suppose he wants to chat, do you?"

"Oh sure. He has so much to say that he cannot wait to blabber."

"Aye. That'll be the day. Why, that old man hasn't breathed a word to anyone—not even to himself—since Moses parted the waters."

"Then what's all his fuss about?"

"Lord only knows," said John Hayward, "but

let's not go over that way to find out. We'll cut across the field here."

With John Hayward leading the way, the pack of boys wheeled to their right, waded through some tall grass and were halfway down the meadow when Samuel realized they had not taken their usual route past the front of his house, but instead ran behind the house to avoid him.

"Come back! Do you hear? Come back, I say! No more pond for you," he cried. And Samuel started after them down the slope, unmindful of the day's heat and his creaking old body.

"Look at that old goat, will you? You'd think his britches were in flames."

"Looks more like he's being massacred by the red men."

Samuel fell, got up, slipped, got up again and continued his downhill flight, waving his arms and screaming at the boys to keep away. By this time, the boys were at the edge of the pond and staring with utter amazement at the sight of old Samuel coming at them.

"If he doesn't stop," said one of them, "he'll run right into the water and drown."

But Samuel did stop.

His ancient frame—at best a sinewy bag of bones—sagged and heaved. He gasped for what little air there was and mopped his brow with the end of his shirt. He tried to say something. But nothing came out of his mouth except the dry gurgling in his throat. Slowly he dragged himself

ιe water and walked into the pond up to his
es, splashing his face with the cool water.

Feeling somewhat refreshed—his face a little
ιss drained of its ruddy color than it had been a
moment ago—he turned and faced the boys, looking squarely at John Hayward and Richard
Spencer who stood slightly apart from the rest
—first one, then the other.

"Get off my land," he began. "Get off and be-
gone with you, all of you and do not come back,
ever."

"It is hot and we aim to stay cool in the water,
put here by the Lord above and not you," shot
back Richard Spencer.

"Keep your peace, Dick boy," said John Hayward. "We shall have the pond and be friends."

"Captain," continued John, using the military
title Samuel was once known by, "Captain, sir,
by your leave, we mean you no harm and never
did you any harm. We have been here many times
before without objection. Pray, sir, why now?"

"Get off my land, I say," Samuel repeated.
"I'll not answer to a mere lad."

"A mere lad is it," answered the boy. And
quickly seeing that Samuel would not be quietly
persuaded, John challenged him: "Muster your
troops, old man, if you mean to stop us. Into the
water, lads! Into the water! Step lively! Look
smart! Quickly now! We stay today and we shall
return tomorrow and every day. Into the water!"

"Aye," someone yelled, "into the water."

"Stout army! Muster my troops," Samuel muttered as he stood knee high in the pond shaking his fist. "Aye, you devils, my army waits for the muster call. We shall see who is the master here."

Soaked, hot, angry, frustrated, less fearful, perhaps, of the discovery of his burial ground and more determined to prove his immortal manhood, Samuel began the long trek uphill to his house and to the musket that silently leaned against the front wall.

When he reached the house, Samuel should have been too exhausted to carry out any threat against the boys. Instead, with wild determination and miraculous strength, he staggered through the door, grabbed the musket and pulled one of the numerous small leather cylinders from a bandoleer that hung from a wall peg nearby.

The old man wheezed as he poured the gunpowder contents of the cylinder down the long barrel of the musket. Then he straightened up, took a deep breath, removed three or four lead balls from a leather pouch and placed them in his mouth. Old Samuel was preparing for battle with the air of a crusty old veteran willing and able to conquer a continent. At this moment, however, Samuel's strategy called for a direct frontal attack to protect his vital interests—the pond and the burial ground behind it.

He ripped the bandoleer from its peg, flung it around his shoulders and stumbled off to make war against the enemy in the pond.

"Here comes old Swift again," cried one of the boys.

"He has a musket! The crazy old fool has a musket!"

No one moved. Every eye was on the armed man coming down the slope. Several of the swimmers stood like sparkling stones—rigid—waist high in water. A few still in deep water softly paddled without going anywhere. Only the gentle ripples of the water crossed the pond and seemed to go somewhere. The boys made no attempt to flee—not out of defiance—but out of absolute astonishment that one old man would actually try to fire upon them. They waited in shocked silence, staring at Samuel's maneuvers in disbelief as if they were caught in a magical trance.

Samuel stopped about halfway down the slope, spit one of the lead balls in his mouth down the barrel, shoved a wad of coarse flax in next and rammed it all home with the vigor of a twenty-year-old soldier. He quickly spun the sparking wheel, aimed the long piece, squeezed the trigger and fired off a round. The kick of the shot knocked him sideways, but he managed to keep his feet and hold onto the heavy musket. The explosion thundered across the pond, echoed into the woods and vanished. The lead ball chewed up an inch of ground and grass ten yards short of the pond. All that remained was the musty, choking smell of gunpowder and a cloud of smoke that hung in the windless air as Samuel tried to regain his balance while trying to spit another bullet down the barrel, forgetting to pour a cylinder of gunpowder and shoving in flax wadding first.

But the old man had no need for a second shot at his startled enemy in the pond. The boys quit the place without waiting to see whether or not Samuel's aim would improve. Samuel watched them go, knowing only too well that they would be back and that he would have to be better prepared to fend them off.

IV

THE BOYS did not retreat very far. Grabbing their
scattered clothes, they ran up the slope, keeping
their distance from the terrible-tempered Samuel,
and faded into a patch of trees. There they quickly
dressed and excitedly held a war council.

"That old man had a mind to kill us all."

"How? With one shot poorly aimed?"

"No! With one shot at a time if we remained."

"He's out of his head with the heat!"

"We can't let him run us off like that!"

"He had the arms. We did not. Besides, the
pond is his."

"His pond or not, musket or not, we still mean
to swim there!"

"Absolutely!"

"What next? Do we cannonade him?"

"Aye. We ought to do just . . ."

"I do not think that old man is trying to kill
anyone," said John Hayward, quietly interrupt-
ing the heated chatter. "He just means to scare
us off."

"Scare us off! Scare us off, you say! Scare us

off what? He never acted like that before. I tell you, Johnnie Hayward, that old man may have missed his mark but he was aiming true enough. I'd like to go right up to his door, take that musket and break it into bits." The angry speaker was William Hampshire, a gruff, barrel-chested youth who could do just that.

"Hold on now, Billie, before you get a ball between your eyes when the door opens," young Hayward replied. "I still think he means to keep us from using the pond short of harming us. He's a bit out of his head, that's all. Maybe the heat has reached his ancient brain."

"Again we say, what next?"

"I think we should give him some of what he tried to give us," continued Hayward, "but not with muskets and shot, mind you."

"Speak up, Johnnie."

"We shall scare the life out of him and maybe he'll not want to venture outside again—least of all take up arms against us."

The prospect of frightening one old man with or without firearms, who could or could not shoot straight, seemed to be very appealing to those Westfallian boys who had just been chased from their watering hole.

"An eye for an eye, a tooth for a tooth," some-one intoned. And for the next hour the boys thought up a number of plans to frighten Samuel Swift enough so that he would not bother them again.

One of the plans called for setting a ring of fire around the old man's house to the accompaniment of loud, weird noises.

"He'll think he's in hell," quipped Richard Spencer, "and that should scare the iron out of anyone, especially an old man like Swift whose time is short."

But that idea was abandoned. It was too dangerous. In all probability much more than twigs and straw would burn up.

Another plan had the boys take up positions all around the house and bombard it with rocks. However, no one could really see the fright in that. Someone said that they should gather all of the cats they could find plus a few dogs and drop them down the chimney during the middle of the night. It did not take much imagination to know what a battleground Samuel would have inside his house. He would have to escape through the front door and that is where the best part of the idea would work. Tumbling through the door, Samuel would come face to face with some frightful apparition—some horrifying figure—perhaps a group of devils with blazing torches; or perhaps some atrocious ghost. At the moment, no one could think up a proper horrible figure with which to confront Samuel and drive him back inside his house forever.

Unable to dream up a good scary idea, the

boys decided to return to the village temporarily. They agreed to meet again after dark at a spot near Samuel's house ready to scare him out of his wits in some manner still undetermined.

V

A FULL MOON was high and bright enough in the starry sky to illuminate the quiet landscape with a pale blue light. Every still form, bush, leaf and tree cast its deep shadow. Swift Pond shimmered with the moon's reflection and at a distance a low yellow candlelight glowed from within Samuel Swift's lonely house.

Slowly all of the creatures of the night began to return to blend their sounds into the nocturnal symphony that serenaded Samuel with the only music he ever knew: the katydids, the frogs, the hooting owls and more. Among them were creatures new and alien to the nightly summer orchestra—the creeping Westfall boys. They had silently approached the rear of the house without so much as cracking a twig. Now they huddled in a compact group as Johnnie Hayward and Dick Spencer crawled toward the house to see what Samuel Swift was doing.

He wasn't doing anything but sitting on his bed.

Soundlessly the boys began crawling back. Not a whisper passed between them. As they reached the huddling group, unseen by any of them, Samuel got up and went out the door. He puttered with some flowers for a few minutes, went back inside to blow out the sputtering candle and then started down the slope toward the pond, his shadow gliding after him like a dark companion.

"I say," someone whispered, "he's put out the candle."

"He's gone to sleep."

"Sleep indeed. There he is!"

"Where?"

"Walking down the meadow."

"What's he up to?"

"How should we know."

"Maybe he's taking his nightly walk."

"Nightly walk!"

"Aye, a nightly walk."

"Have you ever seen him take a nightly walk?"

"Sssssssssh! Keep your voices down."

"No, I've never seen him take a nightly walk."

"Then how do you know he's ta . . ."

"Ssssssssssssssssssssssh."

"Let's follow him and see what he's up to."

"Good idea."

Quickly and silently the boys scattered somewhat and padded after the old man, staying low, behind, and out of sight.

As Samuel reached the pond, he veered to his right, circled around to the other side and entered the woods, an unlit lantern in one hand, some cut flowers in the other.

The boys hurried into the woods at a different point, trying to keep Samuel's moving form in sight while making sure that they remained undetected. They skipped from tree to tree, from bush to bush and shuddered every time a branch snapped or a night bird—probably a bat—swooped past an unsuspecting ear. Samuel was so bent on his melancholy mission, cracking his own dried twigs underfoot as he went along, nothing would have alerted him that anyone was on his trail, watching his movements.

The old man did not go very far into the woods before he reached the clearing. There he stopped. The boys stopped too, not daring to approach any closer. Still unobserved, they could see Samuel furiously trying to get a flame with his tinderbox and light the small lantern. Finally, he was able to strike a spark with the flint and iron that ignited the small piece of rag of the box. He touched the candlewick with the tiny torch and lit his lantern.

The boys could see Samuel a bit more clearly now as he seemed to sidestep a few inches at a time, looking at something on the ground. Suddenly Samuel made some jerking movements with one hand and stood very still talking to himself as if he was conversing with some unseen stranger. The boys could easily hear the mumbling although they could not make out the words.

It was an eerie moment in those humid woods
—a strangely grotesque scene that none of those
Westfall boys had ever witnessed. There in that
moonlit clearing, stark and sharp, stood the
craggy figure of Samuel Swift, crisscrossed by
woodland shadows, apparently alone, doing something, his features glowing and distorted by the
light of the small lantern resting on the ground.
None of the boys moved. Their hearts thumped,
their heads pounded, but none of them moved.
They were sure that Samuel's business was as
dark and foreboding as the night. They did not
want to run. They were adventurers—not cow-
ards.

If by chance they had to run—run for their
lives—they could not, so stiff were they with awe
and chilling fear.

Finally, the mysterious stillness was broken.
Samuel snuffed the lantern candle, moved off in
the direction from whence he came, leaving the
woods, rounding the pond and starting up the
slope. This time the moon was to his back and his
shadow slid before him, seeming to part the
meadow for its master. Samuel was going home.

None of the boys, meanwhile, were willing to
stir until they were sure Samuel was out of range.
Convinced that he was not about to return, Johnnie Hayward directed two of his friends to follow
the old man and make sure.

"See that he's on his way," he whispered, "and
return quickly. Stay out of sight. Old Swift is up

to something and we are going to find out just
what it is."

"You are mad, John Hayward. We ought to
have no business here. These are strange doings.
There is a stink in these trees, the stink of Satan
himself."

"I smell nothing but a snuffed candle and burnt
tinder. Do as I say."

"You heard him," snapped Billie Hampshire,
who had moved closer to Johnnie. "Do as he says
if you want to see the light of day again."

Not wishing to tangle with the likes of William Hampshire whose fists turned to rocks if he
had a mind to use them, the two boys cautiously
followed Samuel's path out of the woods. The rest
remained where they were. It was not long before
the two returned with the news that Samuel was
indeed on his way home and so were they.

"Go if you must," Johnnie told them, his voice
rising an octave with impatience, "and anyone
else who cares to join them." No one budged, not
even the two boys who did not care to remain.
They thought that it would be safer to be among
their friends than to flee through those dark
woods by themselves.

"Now then," Johnnie continued, "we need someone to watch and warn us if the old man changes
his mind and returns."

"I'll do it." The volunteer was short, squat Rob
Whitstone. "But I'll not do it alone."

He was quickly joined by his younger brother

George, whose appearance was not unlike his own, but who shook and shivered with such fright that he could hardly talk. And he was more than happy to be on the edge of the woods rather than inside them where he was sure that all those left behind would never be seen again.

"L-l-l-l-ord h-a-a-a-ve mer-r-r-cy on-n-n y-y-y-ou." And with that blessing, young George gladly turned away from his companions in the night and closely trailed his brother to the edge of the woods—and safety—to watch for Samuel's return.

The half dozen or so boys now in the woods slowly began to close in on the spot where they had last seen Samuel.

"Steady, mates."

No one was steady. And no one seemed to be in a hurry. The nearer they approached the clearing, the tighter the boys clung together.

"Do you smell anything?"

"Nothing but a snuffed candle, I told you. That's all."

"It's hell's sulphur, I tell you!"

"Bah!"

"What was that?"

"What was what?"

"That! There it goes again! It's coming closer!"

"Lord Almighty! I hear it too!"

"Steady, lads. We are almost there."

"Listen! The noise! That devilish sound! It's upon us! God in heaven!"

No, it was not God in heaven who was sending down terrifying noises to split the ears of his mortal children below. Nor was it some devilish messenger sent to destroy their wits with frightful sounds. Neither was it a sound closing in on them as if to fend them off and protect Satan's dark and woody domain. It was an innocent, scruffy owl perched on a thick branch above them as they passed beneath, watching the invaders of his night and property as they had watched old Samuel.

Now they were there. They had come to Samuel's spot in the woods. They backed away at first not knowing what lay hidden, waiting to reach out for them. Then they inched forward, clinging together in a solid mass, swaying this way, then that way, trying to remain upright on a trestle of knocking knees, their thumping hearts wildly mingling with the warm night.

The longer they stood and stared at Samuel's neat row of markers, laced together by the forget-me-nots he had scattered there only minutes ago, the more self-assurance the boys seemed to gain. Driven now by curiosity, they began to unhook their sweaty hands from each other and got on their knees to inspect the markers.

"Look at this! It's a grave marker! I cannot read the name very well. There is not enough light. One name looks to be S-W-I-F-T. Swift!"

"Here's another. And another!"

"And still another!"

"Who are they?"

"Lord only knows. We shall have to wait for more light."

"Not me!"

"One thing is certain. Somebody is buried here."

"Nobody is buried here," exclaimed John Hayward to the startled group. "This ground is not fresh dug. No spade has ever touched it."

"You are wrong, John Hayward. There are markers to say so."

"These prove nothing. I say there is no one in the ground here and never was. These markers are recent and that is why old Swift tried to keep us away today—to prevent their discovery! Sorcery! That's what is going on here! Witchery! I want no part of this place!"

"Nor I!"

"He's coming back! Old Swift is coming back!" The two squatty Whitstone brothers burst upon the group and just as suddenly scattered it.

Dick Spencer picked up a pine branch and breathlessly dusted the dirt around the markers to cover their tracks, before he too fled. He caught up with the rest who were now in full retreat deep in the woods and taking an uphill short cut that would bring them out on the narrow trail that led to Westfall.

VI

By MORNING, every Westfallian knew that something strange had taken place down at Swift Pond during the night. The boys could hardly contain themselves. The village was not so large, nor the people so numerous that news did not immediately circulate everywhere upon receipt. Nevertheless, no one could be sure of what exactly had happened. The boys were so highly charged by their experience that nothing they said made any sense except the words "witchery," "sorcery" and "Satan."

"They have been possessed," cried some of the women. And their daughters wailed in horror at the vision of the flaming souls of the young village boys. Doors were slammed shut and bolted as every family prepared to wait out the devil's appearance in the hope that he would pass them by. But just as quick as they were to bolt themselves in, that is how quick they were to realize their foolishness. The safest place to be was the meetinghouse—the Lord's house. Satan would not dare to put one cloven hoof of his into that place.

As if on command and with one great lurch, every door in the village was flung open and out poured the villagers, running in a large ball of dust toward the meetinghouse. There, waiting to usher them all inside was the imposing figure of elder William Hayward, the leading citizen of Westfall and Johnnie's father.

It was elder Hayward's intention to summon everyone for a meeting not only to find out what had happened—that was the least of it—but to prepare to fight the devil. It was already obvious that Beelzebub had finished his evil work in other villages and was now running amuck down at the pond having first crawled inside the body of old Samuel Swift. And now that everyone was in the meetinghouse, elder Hayward was anxious to get to it.

One by one the boys described the events of yesterday morning. They told how old Samuel fired at them and chased them out of the pond; how they went back to Samuel's house after dark to seek their revenge; how they followed Samuel into the woods; how they watched him; and finally how they came upon the grave markers. But that is where one story ended and another began.

"Then we saw the old man coming back," screeched the breathless, wide-eyed Whitstone brothers. "We were watching for him to warn the others. We saw him all right. We could see right through him!"

"Good Lord," cried their mother.

"More a spirit than a man, he was," they added.

"Aye, we ran," continued Dick Spencer, "but I lingered for a moment to cover our tracks. And then I saw him. It seemed to be old Swift. But his head had no face and his feet were not on the ground. He was being transported by a wind that was not there."

"He was wailing and moaning," declared another.

"And then he . . ."

"Enough, enough," interrupted the entire congregation, "purge the demon from our midst! Purge! Purge! Purge the demon!"

Elder Hayward, too, had heard enough. With one majestic wave of his arm, he silenced the gathering.

"Satan has arrived," he solemnly declared. "He lives in the body of Captain Samuel Swift whose covenant with the Prince of Hell has been of long standing. Who among you can bear witness to Samuel Swift's fidelity to heavenly worship? Who among you can bear witness to Samuel Swift's prayerful offering in this house of worship? And now, my friends, who among you can deny that Satan has come to collect his debt from Samuel Swift?"

No one answered. The silence in the rising heat of the meetinghouse was overwhelming. One middle-aged woman in the rear of the room fainted. Her three daughters desperately tried to wake her up. Someone began to sob. Soon the whole room was wracked with sobs and littered with swooning girls. Hysteria had now overtaken these Westfallians.

Elder Hayward made no attempt to bring the meeting under control until he was ready. He let the noise continue for a few minutes, his eyes burning with excitement. Finally, with another majestic sweep of his arm, he silenced, as before, the weeping congregation. There was no doubt as to the authority of Westfall's leading citizen.

"Now we shall take Samuel Swift, bring him here, exact his confession, drive out his demon and return the Almighty's peace to our homes."

Not one individual stepped forward to begin the march on Samuel Swift. Fear had gripped their holy hearts despite the fierce willingness to battle the devil.

Even Johnnie Hayward who had some doubts about all that he had just heard—John Hayward, the coolest and cleverest of them—decided to believe that Samuel Swift was a menace, acting on instructions of the devil himself. If he and his friends could not frighten Samuel into letting them swim in his pond, the people of Westfall would; and the pond would be theirs to do as they please. Besides, had he disputed what some of his friends had added to the mystery or questioned his father's reason, he would quickly be accused of being in league with the devil. Worse still, he would have to account to his own father for his extraordinary behavior—a father who would show no mercy, not even to his own son, in this the worse crisis to shatter the peaceful history of Westfall.

Finally, after much pleading, elder Hayward was able to convince his congregants that they could not stay in the meetinghouse forever; that some of them would have to go and bring Samuel back to the village to stand trial for whatever acts of sorcery he was sure were hidden in the mysterious doings uncovered by the boys on the previous night. A group of men stepped forward and gingerly offered their services. Elder Hayward then directed his son John to lead some of them to the burial ground, while the others were ordered to capture old Samuel. Everyone else would remain where they were until Samuel was safely locked away.

The two groups marched off—about twenty in all. The first group surprised Samuel as he puttered around his flowers. The old man was so shocked that he offered no resistance. In fact, he was pushed toward the trail that led back to Westfall. There they waited for the second group to finish their business in the woods.

Johnnie pointed out the grave markers to the men who inspected them with some haste. They were not anxious to remain at that spot any longer than was necessary. Nevertheless, they did stay long enough to read the names carved into the bark markers—names they had never heard of before, people they never knew existed. Surely, if any of these lived and died in the Westfall area and were buried in this clearing, how could such events be kept so secret? Stranger still, the group could see for themselves that the ground was undisturbed; that no holes—no graves—had ever been dug there. This alone convinced them that Samuel was involved in some terrible happening, some form of black magic. And in their feverish imagination—imagination dominated by their fear of doom and the uncertainty of their own place in the hereafter—there could be little doubt that Samuel Swift was indeed in debt to the devil. They dared not think how many more like him were heating up the Massachusetts countryside, still free of accusation, casting spells here, there and everywhere. The hot, tiresome weather was a good example.

Quickly they tramped up the slope and joined the others on the march back into the village. Samuel knew what they had found—his burial ground. The old man, his hands tied behind his back, a long, loose rope around his neck, was tugged, pulled and yanked back to Westfall like an animal.

By the time the small column reached the meetinghouse, Samuel was so worn out he could hardly stand. When several of his captors tried to prop him up to face elder Hayward, his accuser, he shouldered them away, spat at one and kicked the other, falling to the ground swearing as Hay-

ward confronted him.

"Samuel Swift, if that is who you are," and Hayward knew only too well that it was, "you have been brought here to answer for your conduct."

Elder Hayward wiped his perspiring face. Samuel got to his feet and glowered at him.

"You stand accused by the good people of Westfall of unspeakable crimes of witchery. In accordance with *our* laws"—and he emphasized "our" as if to confirm Westfall's independence from the rest of Massachusetts—"it is my solemn duty to inform you that you are now under arrest; that you shall be confined to the common jail. There you shall be shackled while the evidence is prepared for your trial. Unless a confession is forthcoming from you now, the days ahead will prove to be most difficult for us all.

"Do you confess?"

"Confess? Confess to what?"

"Witchery," Hayward roared. "Sorcery," he roared again. "Did you not hear my charge?"

"Witchery! Sorcery! You are the devil, not I. I am an old man. Soon to die. I have no powers. Let me go in peace!"

"Do you confess?" elder Hayward persisted.

"No?" he queried Samuel's silence. "Remove this creature from our sight."

PART TWO

THE TRIAL

I

WESTFALL was a speck of a colony within a colony. In 1642, twelve years after the founding of Puritan Boston in the great Massachusetts Bay Colony of North America—and twenty-two years following the Pilgrim settlement at Plymouth— a number of disgruntled settlers decided to leave Boston and make their own way in the wilderness. Calvinists all, strict observers of government by God and the law of the Bible, some fifty or sixty of them—men, women, children—packed up their meager belongings and tramped across the Boston Neck, heaping departing damnations upon those left behind. Boston had become a wanton place for them, a place where men ruled by edicts of their own courts in the service of God but under the supervision of the King of England, not by the will of God alone and His Book of Law. Moreover, the docks of Boston were becoming unrestricted gateways for every kind of seedy sailor and traveler who looked to no law but their own.

Somehow or other these new pilgrims secured a charter and a grant of land for an area west of

Boston from King Charles I, or more accurately, from Charles's rebellious Puritan parliament. The document named the colony *Westfall* "now and forevermore." It also made the Westfallians as independent of the Massachusetts Bay Colony as the Plymouth Pilgrims.

When Plymouth joined the New England Confederation a year later, the Westfallians heaped abominations upon *them,* not that they had not done so before. And when Plymouth cut her last thread of independence in 1691 to become part of the Massachusetts Bay Colony, the Westfallians gathered inside their simple meetinghouse to praise the Lord for keeping them free of Satan and his army—namely the government and people of the Massachusetts Bay Colony, not to mention the rest of the sinning world.

When the service ended, William Hayward's teen-age son John, his only heir, suggested they all gather on the green and celebrate their salvation with a great bonfire.

"Fire!" roared elder Hayward. "Celebration! You, a thin, squeaky boy wish to conjure up in our midst that cloven-hoofed Beelzebub, the master of hell himself, and scorch us all in the sight of God with that devil's own flame!"

And as Hayward spat out his exclamation of horror, the worshipers formed a semicircle before the meetinghouse door. Then quietly, approvingly, they watched the village's leading citizen thoroughly thrash his son. When it was done, elder Hayward looked to the sky, not for forgiveness, but for heavenly sanction, holding the limp boy upright with one great hand and reaching skyward with the other.

"Bear witness, Good Lord," he screamed, "I have purged the demon and his hellish company from this mortal body." And he shook John a little just to make sure the Lord knew to whom he was referring. Suddenly the sky darkened. It began to rain. To some, God must have seen the whipping below. Saddened to tears, He was telling William Hayward and his followers that He, the Almighty, would take care of His fallen angel Lucifer, or Satan, or Beelzebub, or whatever his name was, but that elder Hayward should be more gentle with his son—certainly more understanding of a young boy's enthusiasm. However, elder Hayward received no such heavenly message. It was raining. And it was time to get out of the wet. He dragged his whimpering son back inside the meetinghouse—the Haywards lived in the rear—and slammed the door shut. The satisfied crowd disappeared.

Old Samuel Swift, having made one of his infrequent visits to town, was on his way home when he came upon the commotion at the meetinghouse door. Shuffling slowly by at the edge of the crowd, he saw the cuffing of poor young Johnnie Hayward. The old man suspected that the devil was at the bottom of the scene. Lately, everything in Westfall seemed to wax and wane according to heaven's eternal struggle with hell. Such beatings may have been an effective treatment for exorcising demons and purifying children, but they were happening so often now that no one seemed properly purged of the devil within.

"Children today," he muttered. "Strangers tomorrow."

The old man did not use the word "strangers" lightly. He knew exactly what he meant. During the entire fifty years he lived in Westfall, never once did he attend a religious service inside the meetinghouse or anywhere else. That alone made him a stranger in the eyes of every Westfallian, regardless of how much a familiar part of the scenery he had become. Captain Swift, as he was once known, was an Anglican-born Englishman who went to sea at the age of ten, became a soldier of fortune on the European Continent and eventually came to America for more adventure. Not since he was a small boy did he find time or reason to attend any religious service, except for those of his comrades who died at sea or in some forgotten battle.

Crusty old Samuel was indeed a stranger, who remained unconverted to the faith of the New England Puritans, let alone to those strict ideas that nourished the lives of the people of Westfall. His long-time presence in Westfall was tolerated only because of a business arrangement Westfallians felt honor bound to keep while Samuel Swift lived among them—however long that might be.

At an earlier time, young, muscular Samuel Swift, a fearless professional soldier, was near banishment from Boston. His brawling escapades had become more than Governor Winthrop could stand.

"We must have discipline or we shall not survive," said the governor. "We cannot countenance unbridled behavior of those to whom we have entrusted our lives. Let it be known that one, Samuel Swift, should he again disturb the peaceful intent of the King's colony, be sent away from this place or otherwise be dealt with in a fit and lasting punishment, justly deserved."

Learning of the governor's anger, young Samuel decided it was time to leave—to return to England. Hastily, he signed as a deck hand aboard the only vessel in Boston Harbor at the time, *The Bay of Faith.* A few days later, the ship quit the harbor and set sail for England only to catch fire and sink within full view of the entire Boston settlement. Although badly burned, Samuel jumped to safety and swam the short distance back to Boston. He was the lone survivor of the tragedy, an event that would loom large and ugly in his future.

Hurt and raving, Samuel was carried to the house of Jonathan Hayward where the infant William—that same thrashing, God-fearing William Hayward of later years—was squalling in

his cradle while his mother, Jane, rocked him with the fury of a hurricane. There Samuel Swift was gently restored to perfect health and offered a job.

"The Good Lord had no intention of returning you to the motherland, Samuel," Jonathan Hayward remarked one day. "He has need of you here. We have need of you here. Your good fortune to have lived through the recent disaster at sea was ordained in heaven and with purpose." And then he added, "We are that purpose."

Samuel did not exactly see his rescue in that way, nor did he quite understand what Jonathan Hayward meant by "purpose." However, having been treated with such kindness, he was willing to listen to whatever this new friend of his had in mind.

Hayward then acquainted Samuel with the plan of a number of unhappy Puritans, of which he, Jonathan Hayward was one, to leave Boston for parts unknown under a charter granted to them by the King.

"If you, Samuel Swift, will escort our company of pilgrims to our promised land; if you will oversee the purchase of cannon and other necessities; if you will instruct us in such arts essential for life in the wilderness and otherwise form us up for our own protection; if you will lead us in whatever expeditions shall arise and when threatened by hostile elements; we shall make a home for you among us though you be not one of us. We shall provide you with land, goods and food taken from a common collection. And this we shall do for as long as you will remain in our service. We swear this to you by all that is holy."

Samuel agreed to the offer which he deemed fair, gracious and exciting inasmuch as he had no other choice. He could not remain in Boston under the threat of the governor. He was not interested in attempting another sea voyage. What he did want, however, was to be excused from any religious service and to be left alone when not needed. Jonathan Hayward agreed.

A written agreement was drawn up by the group's Common Council of Elders. Samuel signed the pact which named him Captain and put himself in the service of the Westfall Puritans. His position was not unlike that of Captains John Smith or Miles Standish whose respective colonies, Jamestown and Plymouth, employed them for similar reasons.

On the appointed day of their departure from wicked Boston—an exodus that each and every Westfallian likened to the departure of the ancient Hebrews from Egypt—the Westfall pilgrims knelt in prayer to ask God for safe deliverance. Then, with Captain Samuel Swift, their hired Moses, in the lead, they walked out of Boston hurling their terrible epithets at the jeering spectators who had come to see them go.

Not much changed during the fifty years that passed to soften the feelings between Bostonians and Westfallians. Had Jonathan Hayward lived to a reasonable old age—something no one in Westfall seemed to be able to do except Samuel Swift—things might have been different. But that is only wishful guesswork. In the meantime, Jonathan Hayward's only son, the squalling infant William, had grown to irritable manhood as Samuel Swift drifted into a lonely, friendless old age with no future.

If Samuel had anything at all, it was the knowledge of the excellent service he had given to the people of Westfall for more years than he could remember. But the Council of Elders, whose membership changed very often due to the death or departure of this one or that one, remembered. And although Samuel never became one of their kind, they continued to honor the original contract that put Samuel in their midst so long ago.

And now that business arrangement was ended. Samuel Swift was in jail, accused of witchcraft, awaiting his trial and whatever else the good people of Westfall had in store for him. To every Westfallian—especially elder William Hayward —Samuel Swift simply did not exist any longer. The devil lurked inside him and managed him. He was possessed. The people of Westfall did not feel honor bound to keep an agreement with the devil in the person of Samuel Swift unless, of course, the evil which possessed the old man could be driven out and Samuel became Samuel again.

That was unlikely, however. Samuel was still Samuel—old and confused, perhaps, but still Samuel—and the good people of Westfall had their sorcerer—their warlock. Now they would show the rest of Massachusetts how to deal with such a satanic creature.

11

THE THICK oak door of the one-room jailhouse slammed and locked behind Samuel. Temporarily blinded after the brilliant sunshine from which he had just been thrust, the old man dizzily swayed in the cool darkness that enveloped him, rubbing and blinking his eyes.

Slowly he adjusted to the gloom. He could see the stone floor and rough wood walls. The ceiling was invisible, lost in the deep shadows. There was a bed of straw in one corner; a stone fireplace strewn with wood bowls and plates at the far end; a high tiny window out of reach, too small for a child to squirm through and not nearly big enough for the passage of light. Around his right ankle was an iron cuff connected to a long heavy chain bolted through a floor stone in the center of the room.

Samuel shook his leg once or twice to see if the manacle would slide off. No luck. He dragged himself and his clanking chain to the pile of straw, sank into the soggy, matted sticks and fell asleep, too tired to fully understand the reality of his captivity.

Outside, a small crowd kept a respectful distance from the little jailhouse which imprisoned
the Westfall warlock—the sorcerer as everyone
now called Samuel Swift. To them and to the
rest of the population, Samuel Swift's coming
trial was a formality. They already knew he was
guilty—guilty of living longer than anyone else in
town; guilty of living differently than everyone
else; guilty of prowling the woods at night; guilty
of marking graves that did not exist for people no
one ever heard of; guilty of not worshiping in the
accepted Westfall manner; and worse, still, not
praying to the Lord at all, making it quite plain
that Satan was the object of his worship since
everybody, including Samuel Swift, had to worship one or the other, either the Almighty above
or the devil down below.

The bearded guards stationed on either side
of the door sweated uncomfortably as the afternoon sun made ovens of their iron helmets and
breastplates—pieces of armor that had been rust-
ing in a storeroom for lack of use. The only weapons they had to keep the crowd peaceable were a
couple of crooked pikes. They had no cause for
alarm, however. The collection of fearful people
that stood motionless outside the jailhouse, ob-
livious of the rising temperature of the day,
showed little interest in challenging the guards
or menacing the sorcerer within. As for Samuel,
escape was impossible.

Samuel got little sleep, however. He was jarred

awake about an hour later by one of the guards who poked at him with the sharp end of his pike.

"Arise, you devil you, and stand before the magistrate."

The magistrate was none other than William Hayward, chief citizen, chief churchman, Samuel's principal accuser. He was appointed to his new job not a half hour before at a special meeting of the Westfall Council of Elders. There was no argument, no debate, no opposition, no question as to who Samuel's judge would be. The entire meeting took three minutes. It was always like that. Every time some occasion arose that required the service of a magistrate—Westfall had no permanent magistrate—William Hayward would be appointed in three minutes or less.

"Arise, I say!"

Samuel stood and was promptly shoved to the center of the room. There, magistrate Hayward and his court—the dozen remaining members of the Council—formed a circle and walked around him, looking him over as if, indeed, he was a strangely formed creature from another world. Not a word was spoken.

Samuel twisted and turned as he followed the silent marchers around him. Suddenly he bolted through the moving circle and made for the door, tripping over his chain, which he had momentarily forgotten, and fell against the guard who flung old Samuel to the stony floor.

Hayward leaned over the breathless, shaken

Samuel and asked, "Will you confess or must we
wring the demon from you?"

"You are the demon," Samuel roared. "It is
you who will roast! All of you! What harm have I
brought you?"

"Unhook this sorcerer. Put him in the stock.
Let the innocent look upon this menace. Let them
see what evil lurks in this miserable body."

Samuel was separated from his chain and
dragged outside where his head and wrists were
rudely clapped in the wooden pillory and pad-
locked. Now he stood in the bright hot air squint-
ing at the crowd which appeared to be larger
than before and a bit more restless. No one was
quite sure what would happen next.

A few believed that Satan himself would appear and rescue his servant. Perhaps the Lord of
the Underworld would disguise himself as a great
flame, consume Samuel and burn some of their
number in the process. The crowd backed up a
little. It was hot enough in that dusty, shadeless
place in front of the jailhouse. It was hot enough
for the whole of New England to burn up. Several women sank to their knees and began to
pray. Soon the entire crowd was on its knees praying—magistrate Hayward among them.

Samuel, imprisoned in the pillory, was the
only one left upright. His jaw jutted defiantly as
he surveyed the scene. His mouth seemed to
move as if he was trying to tell them all how mad
they were. But nothing came from his parched

throat. The prayers continued and Samuel sagged, little by little.

"Lord, hear your children. Save us from this wretch," cried one.

Samuel was genuinely shocked to learn that anyone needed to be saved from him. Why, he hardly mingled with these people.

"Lord, protect us from this sorcerer," exclaimed another.

Samuel raged inside with the thought that William Hayward decided he was a sorcerer for no good reason other than to give Westfall something to worry about and to make the town as determined as the rest of Massachusetts in clearing out the devil. And he, Samuel, old, friendless and alone was the perfect target.

"Lord, keep us from his evil spells," added still one more.

Poor old Samuel, he had absolutely no idea that he had ever cast any spells or even knew what a spell was supposed to be. He did recently begin to suspect that his activities down at the pond and in the woods might bring trouble. But as for being evil—casting evil spells—to whom? —over what?

"God Almighty!" cried Samuel finally, "water —give me water—do you hear me?—water!"

That was the first time that Samuel had ever asked God for anything. He surprised himself. The praying crowd was equally aghast that a sorcerer should do such a thing. It never occurred

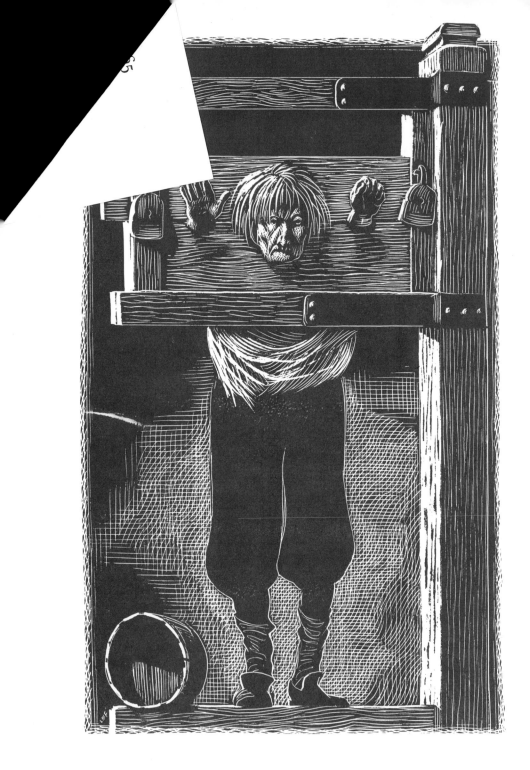

to them that perhaps Samuel was not a sorcerer possessed by the devil.

"It's a trick," someone howled.

"The Lord will not answer to such witchery!"

"Repent. Repent, you damned sinner."

But God's response, if that is what happened next, was immediate and with compassion, if not a bit one-sided. Out of the angry crowd came William Hampshire lugging a bucket heavy with cool, refreshing well water. He dumped it over Samuel. The crowd roared its approval. He then stuck the empty, dripping bucket over the old man's head. Samuel sputtered, wagged his head from side to side and finally shook the bucket off, shrieking with laughter as it rolled away. Drenched, he was cooler in the heat of the withering sun than the steamy throng. Besides, he was a good deal less thirsty than anyone in the crowd, having licked the inside of the bucket while it covered his head.

The old man cackled with glee until he ran out of breath. The crowd understood and made sure that such a mistake would not happen again. Several more buckets of cool water now began to circulate in the crowd. Everyone drank, slaked their thirst and went on praying for their salvation, not Samuel's. And just to show Samuel that he should not expect much mercy for whatever it was the coming trial would surely find him guilty of, a couple of freshly filled water buckets were placed near him where he could see them but could not, in any way, reach out and touch them. Every so often, some villager would come forward and drink from one of those buckets to torment the prisoner. The want of it and the sight of it almost drove Samuel out of his ancient mind. Samuel's shaggy head slowly drooped as he lapsed into unconsciousness.

Several hours later, the blazing, blood-red sun shot one more quivering wave of heat over Westfall and sank out of sight. And Samuel, now partially conscious, mumbling something about "hell's fires," was yanked from the pillory and hauled back inside the jailhouse.

Few Wesfallians were there to see Samuel returned to his prison. Most of them had gone home, too spent to continue their praying vigil. The two or three diehards who had remained had edged closer to Samuel to listen to his mumbling. All they heard was "hell's fires," convincing them that Samuel was somehow in communication with his master, Satan, and that something drastic would have to be done soon before each and every one of them were enslaved by the devil.

In any case, Samuel was tossed on his straw bed like a broken doll. There he was chained, given some stale water, a piece of old bread and a bowl of cold stew which he could not eat. He could hardly raise his head to drink the brackish water let alone swallow the foul stew.

At dawn of the following morning, Samuel was

again roughly jerked from his sleep and prodded to the center of the room to face magistrate Hayward and the others. This time Samuel was too weak to stand and just lay at Hayward's feet.

"What say you now, sorcerer? Is the demon still within you?" asked the magistrate.

"If there be a demon," croaked Samuel, "then I know him to be you."

Hayward ignored the remark and turned to the guard.

"See that he eats and rests. Tomorrow he stands trial. I want him better able to face the charges we shall put to him."

III

THE MEETINGHOUSE was packed to its rafters with anxious Westfallians. Thirteen empty chairs behind a long table awaited the appearance of the Council of Elders, Samuel's judge and jury. The whole place hummed with a murmur of excitement. There was a strain of dire foreboding as well; not over what would happen to the alleged sorcerer, Samuel Swift; not whether he would be found guilty or innocent—everyone knew he had to be guilty of something terrible—it was up to the court to decide what it was and to say so—but what would happen to each and every one of them if Satan should somehow disrupt the hearing, save his servant, Samuel, and cart them all off to a fiery hell where they would remain forever.

A hush settled over the room. Magistrate Hayward followed by the members of his court solemnly entered the room and took their seats behind the long table. A few minutes later, there was dead quiet as Samuel was led into the room by his two guards and shoved into a high-back chair. The guards remained at his side. Samuel never once looked around at the people in the room. Instead, he glared at one man, William Hayward, who was busy conferring with his colleagues at the table.

Presently, one of them, Thomas Surrey, stood up and announced:

"Know ye by all those present, and as God is our witness, that this special court convened by the Council of Elders of the village of Westfall is now in session. The business before this court is to determine the guilt or innocence of one Captain Samuel Swift, with respect to certain charges . . ."

Cries of "witchery," "sorcery," "blasphemy," "idolatry," "guilty" rang from every corner of the room.

"Silence!" screamed Hayward as he slammed his large fist on the table.

And there was silence.

"Certain charges," continued Surrey, "that will in due course be brought before the accused. You will now all rise for the invocation. You, too," motioning to Samuel.

"Dear Lord, we are gathered here this morning in Thy house, in Thine eyes to save our souls. If we have sinned, we repent. Now we ask for Thine heavenly guidance. Help us to see the light of Thine everlasting wisdom. Help us to serve the cause of justice. Help us, Dear Lord, to make this place a decent place for Thy children, not for

1

devils, demons, witches and others who are committed to do eternal battle with Thee. Lord, love us as we love Thee. Amen. Be seated. The accused will rise to hear the charge."

William Hayward pushed his chair back and slowly rose. Looking squarely at Samuel with purposeful arrogance as if to make sure that the full measure of his superiority and influence was not lost on the hapless prisoner, he began:

"Captain Samuel Swift, we the Court of Westfall, sitting in special session this twenty-fifth day of July in the year of Our Lord 1692 and representing the law and the people of Westfall by authority vested in the charter signed and sealed by His Majesty, Charles I, King of all England and Guardian of her dominions," Hayward paused to clear his throat, finding it very difficult to mention the King and the rights of British sovereignty, "do here and now charge you with the following acts perpetrated against the God-fearing citizens of Westfall:

"Assault with a deadly weapon, heresy, treason, witchery.

"How plead you? Innocent or guilty?"

Samuel had to answer for himself. There was no one to help him. He was without benefit of sympathetic advice or any legal counsel. He had no rights whatever. He glanced around the room hoping that someone might step forward and plead for his innocence—for mercy—before such overwhelming odds. But there was no one. As usual, he was alone. Samuel spun around and spat at magistrate Hayward.

"That is my answer to you!"

A guard knocked him to the floor for his insolence and then hoisted him to his shaky feet.

Calmly Hayward asked again, "How plead you?"

"This is all rot," he howled. "I am innocent, I tell you!"

"Do you deny firing your musket at my son and his companions?"

"They were trespassing. I had my rights."

"Do you deny it?"

"No."

"Then you are guilty of that. Mark it in the record, guilty as charged."

"Do you deny not worshiping with our congregation?"

"No."

"Then you are guilty of faithlessness. Mark that down as heresy, guilty as charged."

"Heresy?"

Samuel was plainly shocked at the obvious distortion of his religious indifference.

"I preach no word against the Good Book."

"Heresy we say and heresy it is!"

"Aye," agreed the members of the court.

"Do you deny that you have spoken with the Prince of Hell himself; that you and he conspired to war against Our Lord and Master; and this you have done in the dead of night—an act of treason against the guardians of the one true nation, heaven above?"

"Treason? You are mad with the heat!"

"We have witnesses."

"They are liars!"

"Do you deny practicing witchery as directed by the Prince of Hell in the presence of false graves which you yourself or Satan himself conjured up for what terrible purpose we have yet to learn?"

"False graves? You speak of my family!"

"You have no family and never did! We have dug those graves and found no bones. Nothing!"

"Rot, I say. Rot!"

"We have witnesses to your black doings. Do you still deny? Never mind. Let me tell you," lectured Hayward, growing more irritable, "we have long been wary of your origins. You claim to be an Englishman."

"From London Town," interjected Samuel.

"So you say," replied the magistrate. "You have soldiered for a profession. This we know. Your early life in Boston is also well known to us—an endless procession of wenching, sotting, fighting and intolerable troublemaking of all sorts. You were possessed even then! And how did you come to us? Through a wall of fire! How was it that you alone survived the burning of *The Bay of Faith?* It was said then that the devil was seen in the rigging putting his torch to that goodly vessel. And why were you delivered unto our care?

By what powers were you plucked from that doomed vessel, saved for us, as it were? Were you not born of fire? Were you not weaned on a flame? Who are you—so long tolerated by us—the devil's own instrument or the devil himself?"

A fearful groan rolled across the room as Samuel screamed, "Lies, lies, all lies." But even Samuel had to wonder who he was, so persuasive was magistrate Hayward.

"What is your true purpose here?" continued Hayward. "We aim to know what evil intent is buried beneath that old, wrinkled skin of yours. What spell have you cast over us?"

"I have no purpose. I am no sorcerer. I am a man—an old man. Let me be!"

"How can we let you be when your life is a mystery to us all?"

Magistrate Hayward then abruptly shut off any further dialogue between Samuel and himself.

"This court stands adjourned until sundown this afternoon," he intoned. "The prisoner will be returned to the jailhouse to reflect upon these proceedings and to await our summons."

IV

AT SUNDOWN, Samuel was summoned as promised. The two armed guards dragged him back to the meetinghouse courtroom and pushed him down into the chair facing the long table of the law. The spark, the defiance, all of the enduring vigor of this ancient man which had been present only hours before was gone. He looked wasted and unconcerned. His head rolled around on his bony chest like a heavy ball. He continued to ignore the whispering crowd behind him. He did not look up to glare at magistrate William Hayward as that large, imperious man once again led the members of his court into the meetinghouse to take their seats at the table.

"We shall have witnesses now," proclaimed the magistrate.

One by one, John Hayward, William Hampshire, Robert and George Whitstone, Richard Spencer and several others repeated their versions of the night in the woods.

Those who dug into the burial ground and found nothing buried there were briefly questioned, also.

Actually, magistrate Hayward was not the
least bit interested in witnesses of any kind. Neither were the other twelve members of the court
or anyone else in town, for that matter. Samuel
himself was in too much of a stupor to complain
further about the injustice of Westfall justice.
And if he did complain, little good it would
have done.

Bored after listening to witnesses for only some
twenty or thirty minutes, magistrate Hayward
brusquely ended this part of the trial—if these
proceedings could be called a trial—and turned
to Samuel.

"Now, sorcerer, we wish to know more about
these grave markers."

Samuel was unmoved. He had fallen asleep in
the chair.

A few candles now burned in the steamy room.
Another night was descending on Westfall. Long
shadows danced up and down the meetinghouse
wall as the crowd shifted on the uncomfortably
hard benches. Every so often the flickering light
would drive a few shadows up the wall and onto
the low ceiling where they seemed to converge
and hover above Samuel's head. Under ordinary
circumstances no one would have paid much
attention to these soaring, advancing, retreating
shadows. But in the threatened, frightened imaginations of the hot Westfallians who were near
the end of their endurance of the most withering,
sweltering summer in anyone's memory, these

shadows were not shadows. They were dark, ominous spirits reaching out for Samuel Swift—or maybe for *them,* the God-fearing people of Westfall.

Little by little, every eye became fastened to the ceiling—to the leaping rhythm of the shadowy dance that became more agitated, more pronounced as dusk became night—black and mysterious—and the flickering candles burned brighter, more intensely. None of this was lost on the thirteen judges, not even the relentless, unforgiving master of them all, magistrate Hayward. He too, fixed his stare on the ceiling and saw it all as a dreadful sign of Samuel's evil doings, and that none of them were safe from his sorcery, not even in the meetinghouse, the last place in town that one could seek the Lord's protection.

Hayward would not be cowed by witchery, however. He was determined to terrorize old Samuel. Yet, it was plain to see that the magistrate had become unsettled by what he surely thought were powerful adversaries unleashed by Satan himself—those shadows. Addressing himself to the prisoner whose head still lolled about on his skinny chest, but faltering somewhat, the magistrate continued,

"Do—do you deny making these markers?" Slowly he looked up at the shadows overhead. "These—these monuments to no one?"

The uneasy courtroom waited for an answer. None came.

"Do you deny," Hayward's mouthed dropped open as he gaped and swallowed hard at the sight of a particularly rapid movement of the shadows above, "their unholy purpose?"

Again, silence.

"Speak up, sorcerer! Answer the questions!"

"He's asleep, sir," said a surprised guard.

"Asleep! Impossible! Humbug!" And pointing to the ceiling, Hayward leaped out of his chair, shouting, "He is dealing with those demons!"

"Aye," sighed the crowd, which by this time was too terrified to either leave the questionable safety of the meetinghouse and return home, or remain where they were. They were caught, trapped in this hellish nightmare from which their only release was the absolute destruction of the alleged sorcerer in the courtroom, Samuel Swift.

"Be done with it!" someone roared.

"Hang the devil!"

"To the stake!"

"Death for the witch!"

The guard jabbed his pike at Samuel's shoulder several times, ripping what was left of the old man's shirt sleeve. It was more of a nudge than a jab. It was not sharp enough to break Samuel's old hide. But in the changing light, it appeared to those closest to Samuel—magistrate Hayward, several others behind the table and a half dozen more seated on the first bench—that the metal point had gone into Samuel's shoulder and out again without so much as drawing a drop of blood.

William Hayward flattened himself against the back of his chair, staring in disbelief at what he thought he had just witnessed—a bloodless wound, the only hard evidence needed to tell them that Samuel was a bloodless creature, the mark of a witch. The others gulped and drew back.

Hayward seized upon the moment and boomed, "He is bloodless, I tell you! Bloodless! He is a sorcerer! Satan himself! I have seen it with mine own eyes! He is guilty! Guilty! Guilty!"

"Guilty!" echoed the crowd. "Guilty! Guilty!"

The guard jabbed Samuel again, this time a little sharper. Still no skin was broken. Still the impression in that misleading light was that of a penetrating wound.

"Look!" cried Hayward. "It happened again." Hayward seemed more elated and pleased than shocked at actually witnessing something no one else in his right mind or in all honesty had ever seen.

One more jab and Samuel suddenly jerked his head up and glassily looked at his accuser and judges.

"The ship is burning," he groaned hoarsely. "There's fire in the fo'c'sle. Got to get out. Got to get off." Samuel blabbered on about his surviving the burning *Bay of Faith* so long ago, but his words trailed off into a seeming senseless mixture of sounds.

"What's that? What did he say?" asked magistrate Hayward.

The two guards leaned close to Samuel and listened to the strange but steady stream of garbled words that Samuel mumbled just above a whisper.

"Can't understand him, sir," said one. " 'Tis a strange language, indeed."

"It sounds like there is a fire someplace," said the other.

"Strange language, is it!" replied the magistrate. "Bring him here."

The guards dragged the still blabbering Samuel before Hayward who leaned forward to listen.

Samuel, who had now broken down under the stress of his ordeal and was quite incoherent came face to face with William Hayward who was a victim—as was everyone else in the room—of his own beliefs and terror-struck fantasies. One was out of his mind with age and longing; the other was out of his mind with fear and power.

"I hear him well," Hayward shouted to the packed gathering. "This is no strange language. While I cannot understand a word, I assure you it is the satanic tongue. This sorcerer, even now, converses with the devil!"

A great clamor rose from those hard benches. And Samuel blabbered on.

"Away with him!"

"Hang him now!"

"Enough," ordered the magistrate. "We shall

do what is right in accordance with the law." Quickly the thirteen-man tribunal conferred and decided not to carry on this trial any further. Samuel was guilty and had to die without delay. To continue would only risk certain doom for everyone.

The short conference ended and magistrate William Hayward stood before the assemblage and proclaimed what they had all expected to hear:

"Captain Samuel Swift, we the Court of Westfall, representing the law and the people of Westfall by authority vested in the charter signed and sealed by his Majesty, Charles I, King of all England and Guardian of her Dominions," again Hayward had trouble mentioning the King of England, "and as God is our Witness, find you guilty of all charges and sentence you to be hanged by the neck—for crimes of heresy, witchery and sorcery—until dead. The aforesaid sentence will be carried out at ten o'clock tomorrow morning, July 26, in the year of Our Lord 1692, at that place called Pilgrim Oak. From there your remains will be removed and deposited in the unknown woodlands without benefit of ceremony—which you hardly deserve—or monument. May the Lord have mercy on your . . . no, strike that last sentence from the record."

Samuel, during all of this, kept up his steady stream of low, jumbled noises. He was completely unaware that he had just been summarily convicted of witchcraft and sentenced to die some twelve hours hence. As he was being led out of the meetinghouse, he unaccountably paused at the door, whirled around to face the packed room and howled with all the strength he had left, the name of his brother, Nathan.

It was the last time that Samuel Swift would say an intelligible word. The next day, at exactly ten o'clock in the morning, the crusty, broken old soldier, was hanged at the place called Pilgrim Oak.

Only the summer heat, more insistent than ever before, continued to plague the God-fearing people of Westfall.

PART THREE

WESTFALL REVISITED

I

A CARPET of restless autumn leaves covered the ground around Westfall. Once in a while the crisp October wind would scatter a few to some distant corner or against a nearby fence where they would remain undisturbed, out of reach of the pursuing wind. The cool, dry air of fall seemed to belie the hot oranges, reds and bright yellows that glittered from the dying landscape, only recently thick with the growing green of summer. Summer's blistering heat was not even a memory in Westfall. Only the passion produced by that heat—the hanging of the Westfall warlock, Samuel Swift, ancient sorcerer—was all that was left to remember and talk about. That was a triumph—Westfall's victory over Satan—a triumph worth remembering and talking about.

No one noticed the two horsemen trotting their mounts easily past the meetinghouse. They had come and gone in a gust of wind and swirling leaves down the road that led to Samuel Swift's vacant house.

It was Sunday. Everyone was in the meetinghouse fervently praying and thanking the Good Lord for all of His kindnesses; most especially His most recent kindness in which He saved them from a certain eternal calamity with the devil. Yet, however much they addressed themselves to Our Lord and Protector, no one was quite sure how far He would go in keeping them out of harm's way and protect them from any further satanic terror.

None of the boys went near the pond—now that it was free and clear—since old Samuel was executed. Nor did anyone venture too close to Samuel's—that is, *the late* Samuel's house. Soon after the old man was hanged and buried in a scrubby patch of woods together with his markers, the Council of Elders ordered that his property, house and belongings be turned over to the town of Westfall. But the town's governing body, the Council of Elders, made no effort whatever to claim any of it.

A few weeks later, the council decreed that a public auction be held for the sale of the property and belongings. They named one of their own, elder Thomas Crawford, auctioneer. But no one came to the auction, not even the auctioneer. Obviously, no one wanted to get too close to the Swift house which was now assumed by everyone to be bewitched.

After a while, someone suggested that the sorcerer's house be burned to the ground, including everything inside. But no one wanted to do it. A few said that it would be a waste of time to try and put the torch to the house of a sorcerer— living or dead—since such a house was under the protection of the devil and could not possibly burn. The rest feared that Satan himself would appear in the flames to seek his revenge among those who dared to destroy one of his companions and the house he used to live in.

Sooner or later something would have to be done. But not now. Now, some two and a half months since Samuel's arrest, trial and hanging, fear still compelled the people of Westfall to move with extreme caution. A few villagers began to think that perhaps it was not such a good idea to execute the sorcerer—or at least, not so hastily. Only one of them, Johnnie Hayward, had the courage to say so and his own father, William, had him put in the stock for a day to mend his ways. No one thought out loud again.

In any case, none of these events and uncertainties were known to the two horsemen who rode surprisingly unnoticed amid the flying leaves, disappearing in the direction of the late Samuel's house. One of the riders was a burly, middle-age man who seemed heavier, bigger and stronger than the sagging, puny horse he sat on. The other was an ancient, skinny old man who was as bony as his mount and who looked enough like the late Samuel Swift to be a close relative, as indeed he was—Nathan Swift, Samuel's brother. It was the very same Nathan whose name Samuel had bellowed in one last fit of clarity and strength as he was led from his trial and conviction to await his punishment. Nathan, the brother, who was last seen on a Thames River dock in London sixty-two years ago and never heard from again—until now. Nor did *he* ever hear from Samuel again, for that matter. Nathan had come out of the dim past in seeming answer to his brother's call, however late. And how strange it was that Nathan Swift and his friend began their journey on the morning of Samuel's execution—a difficult, perilous journey that would bring them to Westfall ten weeks later from a spot on the Connecticut River, not fifty-five miles west of Westfall!

NATHAN SWIFT'S sudden and belated appearance in Westfall may have been somewhat astonishing after all that had happened, yet, his presence in Massachusetts was not so extraordinary. Actually, he had been in New England for twenty-five years, wondering from time to time—but not too often—what had happened to his younger brother since they had last said good-by almost a lifetime ago. Although he could never be sure, Nathan had long ago concluded that the adventuresome, brawling Samuel had come to an untimely end, a victim of some forgotten violence on a patch of land or sea yet to be discovered, and let it go at that.

Nathan's life, on the other hand, was tied to events that were not of his own making. One of these events, strangely enough, was an enormous fire that drove him clear out of England and on to the New England coast. Fire! The devil's own instrument, according to many, most especially the people of Westfall, Massachusetts, a place Nathan Swift never heard of.

Briefly, Nathan, a sailmaker by trade, lost his

wife of thirty years during the awful plague that struck garbage-strewn London in 1665. Childless Mary Swift was one of seventy-five thousand or more Londoners who died in that catastrophe. Nathan was fifty-eight years old at the time and by his reckoning was the last of the living Swifts.

The following year, a great fire ravaged London. More than thirteen thousand buildings— wooden buildings—were burned to the ground. At least fifty thousand people were left homeless, jobless, destitute, no place to go. Nathan Swift was one of them.

Undaunted, and having no further ties to the land of his birth, Nathan joined the crew of a small Boston-bound vessel and came to America. Instead of landing in Boston, however, he came ashore at the mouth of the Connecticut River near the settlement of Saybrook, the ship having been blown off course by a relentless January storm.

From that first day in America and for the next twelve or thirteen years, Nathan wandered up and down the Connecticut River. He grew some corn in Saybrook for a time and then settled in the Massachusetts colony of Springfield. He was there, in Springfield, when an army of Wampanoag Indians led by their chief, Metacomet, who the colonists called King Philip, attacked and burned the place. Nathan managed to escape and fled farther up the river to Northampton. Several years later—about 1680—Nathan came back down river again and settled permanently at Holyoke on the river's western bank, about halfway between Northampton and Springfield.

It was in Holyoke, a dozen years later, during the unbearable heat wave of July 1692, to be exact, that Nathan Swift met Edward Small. Small had come to Holyoke from Dedham in search of a new place to live. He had left his wife and six children behind until he could find a proper tract of land to suit his purpose. Dedham itself was a small village near Boston and not far from Westfall. Small knew all about Westfall— its history and inhabitants—although he had never been there and had never personally met its people.

One sweltering day the two men sat in the shade of a towering elm and talked of the witchery that infected Massachusetts. Small related what he knew about the goings-on in Salem of which Nathan had heard nothing. Small's report casually drifted to Westfall, wondering what, if anything, was happening there.

"Sooner or later," he remarked, "those Westfall people will find enough demons to make Salem and all the rest look like pleasure gardens. Satan himself had better walk softly in that place. They are a strong-willed, stiff-necked, God-fearing lot, they are. I'll wager there is not one soul in Westfall who would dare cross a fellow they call elder Hayward who rules the place like he was a holy king."

Edward Small paused for a moment and then added, "Well, all, that is, except one old man who lives alone and out of their way. Why, he's not even a churchgoing man, I hear. He's different. I think his name is Swann or Swain—no—Swift—that's it—Swift—same as yours."

Nathan was startled.

"Does he have a Christian name?"

"I suppose he does. But I do not know it."

"What does he do there? Where does he come from?" Nathan was quickly becoming more anxious.

"All I know," replied Small, "is that he used to be a wenching, quaffing, troublemaking seaman who was thrown out of Boston. He thereupon joined a number of pilgrims leaving Boston for a chartered place to be called Westfall and who were badly in need of the services of a man-of-arms. He performed goodly service over the years and so they tolerated him among them."

While Edward Small did not have his facts straight, there was enough truth in what he said to give a reasonable description of Samuel Swift's essential character and situation.

Small related a bit more of Westfall's early history, as best he could, continuing to twist some of the truth but maintaining a fairly accurate picture over-all.

Nathan began to reason over the next few days that this man Swift now in Westfall might very well be his brother. He became agitated and pleaded with Small to take him to Westfall when he, Small, returned to Dedham. Nathan explained his anxiety and the possibility of the reunion that awaited him in Westfall.

Small, for his part, was ready to leave immediately. He had found the land he sought. He had built a small house to serve his family temporarily. Now he was ready to return east to fetch them. But Edward Small would not return by the short overland route—the way he had come. It was too dangerous. He preferred a water route, however long that would take.

"It is a long journey for one so old as you, Nathan. You will perish before we are three days gone. Do you still want to go?"

"I must. I must try. If I perish, so be it. God will decide."

On the morning of July 26—the very morning Samuel Swift was hanged for his alleged crimes of witchery—Nathan Swift and Edward Small pushed a raft into the Connecticut River, jumped aboard with a few belongings and slowly began to drift and pole their way south to Saybrook, arriving there several days later.

They lingered impatiently in Saybrook for two weeks until a small trading sloop took them along the coast, through Nantucket Sound, around Cape Cod, into Massachusetts Bay and finally Boston. The little vessel made more stops than either Nathan Swift or Edward Small could later remember. She put in at every tiny settlement that

dotted the coast and riverways—sometimes staying two or three days while the captain went about his trading business.

The trip along the edge of the Atlantic Ocean took five uneventful weeks. The water was still and flat, the air nearly windless. On several occasions there was no wind at all and the vessel, becalmed between Block Island and the Elizabeth Islands, drifted helplessly toward the open sea. Each time, however, she was rescued by a hot breeze and set back on course. By the time Nathan and his companion had reached Boston, summer had turned to autumn.

For some unaccountable reason, both men spent another week in Boston before setting out on a couple of tired old horses for Dedham, only a day's ride away. Finally, they reached Edward Small's house where his family was overcome with joy at his unexpected and unannounced arrival. There Nathan rested his weary body for three or four days while Small made inquiries about Westfall and "that man Swift."

All that he learned was Swift's given name—Samuel, the location of Samuel's house, and that someone in Westfall had been accused of witchery, that a trial had been held sometime ago, but the outcome was unknown to anyone living outside of Westfall.

"Neither Massachusetts nor the Crown are privileged to know what happens there," one of

Edward Small's distant neighbors sarcastically remarked. "They are unto themselves. And for our
part, we concern ourselves not!"

Armed with no more than what they had just
learned, Edward Small and Nathan Swift rode
out of Dedham. Two days later, on this blustery
October Sunday morning, they trotted past the
Westfall meetinghouse unseen by the worshiping
throng inside or anyone else who might have been
about. Shortly afterward, Nathan burst into the
empty house of his late brother while Edward
Small tethered the horses.

III

SUNDAYS in Westfall were quiet and peaceful. This particular Sunday was no different—at least for most of the day. The place seemed deserted. Nothing stirred except the wind and the restless leaves. No one could be seen anywhere. With the final "amen" of the morning's religious service at the meetinghouse, everyone shook hands, went home to observe the Sabbath and stayed there. They did little but eat, sleep and read from the Scriptures, either silently or to each other.

At the Swift house on the western edge of the village, a short column of smoke rose from the stone chimney before the gusty wind took it and whipped it around and around, back and forth until it gradually vanished in the clear air. Occasionally, a strong gust would beat the smoke back down the chimney or not let it escape at all, sending clusters of snapping sparks and clouds of soot and ashes into the room. The two travelers, who had built the fire, gasped and choked but continued to sit by the roaring blaze as they became increasingly concerned about Samuel Swift's absence—a lengthy absence as they could plainly see by the appearance of the place. The door had been left wide open. The house smelled musty and unlived in. There had not been a fire in the fireplace for months. A musket near the door was beginning to rust. There were other signs of vacancy as well.

During the late afternoon, as Nathan and his companion talked and waited, and as the smoke continued to curl up the chimney to meet the brisk outdoors, muscular William Hampshire decided that he had had enough of the Sabbath. The youth quietly stole out of his house—the first between the Swift house and the rest of Westfall —as his parents slept. Quickly he headed toward a wooded area where he hoped to have some sport and catch a wild turkey with his bare hands.

Billie knew a great deal about the forests and streams around his house and other parts of Westfall. So did everyone else in Westfall. But few could ever boast—as did Billie and his friends, John Hayward, Richard Spencer and several others—of one special adventure in the woods which led to the capture and hanging of a sorcerer.

Loping along on the dry ground, Billie spied the wisp of smoke reaching above the treetops. He could see the Swift house and its stone chimney from which it came. He stood behind a tree, motionless, watching the silent, drifting smoke through the naked branches and falling leaves, wondering whether or not he should approach the house and see who was there. Surely, he thought, no one from Westfall would dare enter that forbidden place, let alone build a fire in its fireplace.

The fact of his passing so close to that house had already unnerved him somewhat. He knew that he had no business being there in the first place, chasing wild turkeys on the Sabbath. He began to wish for a companion.

"If only Johnnie-boy were here," he muttered.

But little by little he began to move forward, almost without realizing it; pushed by the invisible power of his own curiosity and sprouting manhood. Billie Hampshire was no coward.

His feet were heavy with misgiving as he stepped behind trees and melted into the brush. The closer he got to the house, the less sure he was of wanting to find out who was inside. He began to remember altogether too many tales of witches and warlocks, devils and goblins who refused to die no matter how often they were put to death, always returning to the magical houses in which they lived and from which they cast their eternal spells.

But Billie went on, inch by inch, until he reached a window. There he sat, underneath, his back against the clapboards, mustering the great courage he needed to look into that window.

IV

BILLIE got to his knees, turned around and faced the wall. He was shaking and fearful but still not willing to run without knowing who was in the house. And now was the time. Night was coming. The sun would soon drop from its perch in the western sky. He pressed himself hard against the building and slowly, steadily began to rise.

As his eyes came over the sill of the dirty window, he could see two figures. One was a stocky man standing with his back to the fire. The other was an older man, seated on a bench and facing the fire. Billie could hardly make out their features although there seemed to be something vaguely familiar about the seated figure. The standing man's features were silhouetted against the sharp light of the crackling fire; while the seated man had his back to Billie.

Presently they stirred.

Edward Small turned and jabbed at the fire with a long iron fork. The fire crackled, sparked and brightened. Now Billie had a better look at him. The flickering light that lit up his face, the fork and the rest of him gave Edward Small a devilish appearance, however. Billie knew that he had never seen him before and in a fleeting moment was not quite sure he ever wanted to see him again.

While Small continued to poke at the fire, Nathan Swift stood up, stretched and began to pace the creaky floor. As the firelight danced across Nathan's tired old face, Billie gasped. In that sharp moving light, Nathan's resemblance to his late brother, Samuel, was uncanny. As far as Billie was concerned he *was* Samuel. The horrified youth fell to the ground and lay there, his face buried in a pile of dry leaves, his head and heart pounding wildly.

"My God," he groaned, "it's the old goat! It's the sorcerer! He's come back from the dead! Oh Lord! And he's got the devil with him!"

Billie was too paralyzed with fear to move. He wanted to run but he could not get up. He began to sob. Finally, he forced himself to scramble on all fours well away from the house and with mounting hysteria fled all the way home.

Billie's mother and father, long since awakened from their Sabbath afternoon nap, were now awaiting his return, ready to punish him for his Sabbath escapade—whatever it was. But when Billie crashed through the door, dirty, cut, bruised, his clothing torn, his eyes wide with terror, sobbing and sighing uncontrollably, his parents knew that something dreadful had happened.

They had all they could do to quiet their son,

bring him to his senses, at least enough to learn the cause of his sobbing distress. They managed to quiet him down after a while, but never again would Billie Hampshire be brought to his senses altogether.

"I saw him," he whimpered. "I saw him. With my own eyes I saw him!"

"Who did you see?"

"The sorcerer himself! Samuel Swift! Alive! In that house of his! And he had the devil with him!"

"Impossible!"

"I saw the both of them, I tell you!"

"Samuel Swift and the devil?"

"Aye. And what a terrible sight it was! The whole inside of the place was bright with hell's fire. The devil stood there laughing and stoking his fire, making the old sorcerer march up and down like the soldier he was. Oh Lord! You should have seen old Swift's face—angry it was! They'll be coming for us, I tell you!"

"Samuel Swift is dead and buried," thundered his father, "and you are raving."

"Go see for yourself," snapped Billie. And with that he broke into another fit of sobbing. His mother flopped on a stool and vacantly stared into space, wide-eyed, open-mouthed, limp—resigned to the horrible fate that awaited them all.

Billie's father grabbed a garden hoe—for whatever good that would do—tore out of the house and headed straight for the Haywards with the unbelievable news.

As much as elder Hayward saw the possibility in what Billie's father told him, he was, nevertheless, gripped with fear at the awesomeness of such a calamitous event.

Clutching his Book of Psalms, the only handy weapon he considered formidable enough to keep the devil and Samuel Swift out of Westfall, and trailed by his son, Johnnie, and Billie's hoe-wielding father, elder Hayward quietly roused several others nearby. The little band, armed with assorted weapons—a Bible, a couple of muskets, a rake, a sword and some heavy sticks—soon closed in on the Swift house. One by one, they peered through the window unobserved where they saw very much the same scene as Billie Hampshire had seen and described.

Convinced, too, that the two men inside were Samuel Swift and the devil, they quickly retreated in a state of shock not knowing what would happen next and what, if anything, they would or could do whenever what might happen, happened.

Night had now fallen. The brightly glowing house with its two occupants stood in vivid, quiet contrast to the blackness that enveloped the apprehensive Westfallians. The awful news of the return of Samuel Swift, the sorcerer—the Westfall warlock—had shattered the peace of every family in the village. Those brave enough joined elder Hayward and the others as they waited in the dark, cold night. The rest sought the safety of their prayers in the meetinghouse.

For a long while, everything seemed to be frozen in time. Nathan Swift and Edward Small, inside the house, seemed to be motionless by the light of the fire. Not even their horses, tied to a tree on the other side of the house, completely hidden from anyone's view, made any noise or movement. Elder Hayward and his watchful militia kept a stony silence. Only the occasional sound of praying voices drifted overhead with the wind.

Suddenly, without warning, the light inside the house turned considerably brighter. The two figures could be seen scurrying about. Within seconds, the whole place burst into flames. Edward Small had jabbed the burning wood in the fireplace once too often. A shower of sparks and hot chinks vaulted past him and ignited some straw. Quickly the dry old house began to crumble in a snapping, wind-whipped mass of fire.

For a brief moment or two, Nathan and his friend could be seen through the wall of flames by the crowd of Westfallians who had kept their vigil. But in that brief moment, Nathan Swift had come to the end of his long journey—a journey that held the promise of a reunion of brothers so long lost to each other. Nathan would never know how close he had come to Samuel's late and unlamented life. Nathan Swift perished in his brother's flaming house.

Edward Small escaped after having tried first to pull Nathan free of the house. Failing to do so, his clothes on fire, Small managed to get outside where he rolled on the ground to put out his own fire. Thinking he had done so, but only partially succeeding, he freed the horses, mounted one and rode off down the slope toward the pond. He had no idea that there was a pond at the bottom of the slope and just permitted the panic-stricken horse to go its own way. Luckily the pond was there. Both Small and the horse fell into its icy water and extinguished what was left of the fire on his back. Several days later, Small returned home. Strangely, he had survived the episode without a scratch or single burn on his body. He told his wife what had happened. They were deeply moved by the death of Nathan Swift who Small had admired but were very thankful for Edward Small's survival. Small never again mentioned the burning house, which by then had been reduced to ashes. Such incidents—the destruction of a lonely house by an adventurous fireplace spark— was a common occurrence in early New England. The following spring, the Smalls of Dedham moved to Holyoke as planned.

In any event, seeing the still burning Edward Small and a horse go galloping toward the pond, toward the imaginary burial ground where the saga of Westfall's battle with Satan began, the watching crowd became at once alarmed and terrified. Now they were sure that they had seen the devil himself and were at the beginning of their untimely end. Had they been able to see Small, soaking wet, rise out of the pond, they might have thought more rationally about all that was going on.

Instead, terrorized by the idea that Samuel Swift was now preparing to march through the flames filled with terrible revenge for what had been done to him and drive them all into the arms of the devil who waited for them in the woods at the burial ground, the watching crowd ran for their lives, dropping their Bibles, sticks, hoes, muskets, swords and whatever else they had armed themselves with.

Those at the meetinghouse had seen the night sky come alive with the reddish glow of the fire. Now they heard the howling, frightened and disorganized mob come racing toward them, chased by nothing but their own imaginations. But the praying continued, much louder, much stronger, as many in the mob thundered past the meetinghouse and kept on running clear out of Westfall. They were never seen or heard from again.

There were those in that fearful, racing mob who stopped long enough to yank their loved ones from the meetinghouse and then continued the flight from Westfall. There were those who did not bother to stop for a wife or daughter or son.

By midnight, not a living thing remained. Every man, woman and child, every cat and dog, the pigs, the hens, the roosters, the cattle, even the songbirds, everything that breathed was gone from Westfall—swallowed up by the miles of surround-

ing wilderness. Nothing was ever heard from or about them again.

In fact, not even the town itself remained. It too disappeared from the face of the New England earth!

For several days after the flight, fire ravaged most of the village. Nearly all of the fleeing families had left candles burning in their wooden houses and fires still roaring in their fireplaces. Needless to say, many of these dwellings burned down to the ground just as easily and just as quickly as the Swift house. Those few buildings that did remain—the meetinghouse, the jail, one or two houses and a gristmill—stood empty and ghostly for another week when a violent unseasonal thunderstorm shook the place.

Lightning struck the meetinghouse and set it ablaze. Fanned by a cold wind, the fire spread everywhere until all of what remained was a heap of charred wood, ashes and blackened stone. Not even the driving rain could diminish the force of the fire. By the following summer there was not a trace of Westfall. The wilderness had grown over it. In time to come, crowded, modern civilization would overwhelm the spot once called Westfall and no clue would ever be found that Westfall—the overgrown ruins of Westfall—lay buried underneath.

It was as if Westfall and her people, Samuel Swift and the others, never really existed to begin with.

Perhaps not.

Whatever the truth of the matter, someone, something came to Westfall and destroyed it. And Samuel Swift and all the rest were innocents caught in some titanic battle between invisible powers.

Or were they?

LEONARD EVERETT FISHER, painter, illustrator, author and educator, was born and raised in New York City. His formal art training began at the Heckscher Foundation in 1932 and was completed, after his wartime military service, at the Yale Art School, from which he received a Master of Fine Arts degree and the Winchester Fellowship. He had studied previously with Moses Soyer, Reginald Marsh, Olindo Ricci and Serge Chermayeff. In 1950, Mr. Fisher received a Pulitzer Art Fellowship. He spent much of that year in Europe, returning home in 1951 to become dean of the Whitney School of Art in New Haven, Connecticut. He resigned from that post in 1953 and turned his attention to children's literature. Since then he has illustrated approximately two hundred children's books, about twenty-five of which he has written, including *The Death of Evening Star*. He has received numerous citations, and in 1968 he was awarded the Premio Grafico for juvenile illustration by the International Book Fair, Bologna, Italy—the only American thus honored. Books containing his illustrations have been published in a variety of foreign languages and distributed throughout the world by the United States Information Agency. Mr. and Mrs. Fisher and their three children live in Westport, Connecticut.

PBK   FISHER   37780
             WARLOCK OF WESTFALL

DATE DUE			